Paddington had lots of presents, but his favourite one of all was a conjuring outfit from Mr. and Mrs. Brown. It came from Barkridges and it not only had a table and a large box for making things disappear, but there was a special magic wand and a book of instructions as well.

Unfortunately, before he had time to try out any of the tricks, the guests began to arrive and he hurried downstairs to greet them.

MICHAEL BOND

Paddington's
BIRTHDAY PARTY
Illustrated by Barry Wilkinson

COLLINS COLOUR CUBS

No one, not even Paddington, knew quite how old he was when he arrived at number thirty-two Windsor Gardens, so the Browns decided to start again and call him "one".

Everyone agreed with Mrs. Bird when she said they ought to celebrate the occasion by holding a birthday party.

His friend, Mr. Gruber, who kept an antique shop in the market, was the first to arrive, and he was closely followed by the Browns' bad-tempered neighbour Mr. Curry.

Mr. Gruber was always welcome, but Mr. Curry hadn't even been invited.

"I bet he's only after the free tea," hissed Jonathan.

Luckily Mrs. Bird's teas were usually so ample there was more than enough for everyone — including uninvited guests. So even Mr. Curry had no cause to complain.

In fact, everyone voted it the best tea they'd ever had, and Paddington himself was so full he had a job finding enough breath to blow out the candle. But at last he managed it without singeing his whiskers, and everyone clapped and wished him a Happy Birthday.

After tea, Paddington announced that he had a special surprise for everyone. Then he disappeared upstairs to his room in order to get ready for it.

While Mrs. Brown and Mrs. Bird cleared away the tea things, Mr. Brown set about arranging the rest of the guests at the other end of the room.

No sooner had everyone settled down than the door opened and Paddington reappeared, staggering under the weight of his magic outfit.

"Ladies and gentlemen," he announced, when all was ready. "My next trick is impossible."

"But you haven't done *one* yet!" called Mr. Curry.

Paddington ignored the interruption. He consulted his instruction book.

"For this trick," he continued, "I would like an egg, please."

Mrs. Bird looked worried. "Oh, dear," she said. "Can't you use something else?"

"No," said Paddington firmly. "It definitely says an egg. I'm going to turn it into a bunch of flowers," he added darkly, ". . . if I can get my magic wand to work."

Paddington held up the magic wand and began making some passes over it with his other paw. To everyone's astonishment, including his own, it suddenly went quite limp.

"Quite good for a bear," said Mr. Curry over the applause. "Of course we all know it's joined by elastic in the middle . . . but quite good."

Paddington gave the Browns' neighbour a hard stare, but luckily Mrs. Bird came into the room at that moment carrying an egg.

"Do be careful," she warned. "I had the carpet cleaned only last week."

Paddington thanked Mrs. Bird, and then placed the egg on his magic table and covered it with a handkerchief. "Now," he announced, "if you watch closely you will see it turn into a bunch of flowers."

"I'd sooner you turned it into an omelette," called Mr. Curry. "I'm getting hungry again."

But Mr. Curry's words fell on deaf ears,
for Paddington was much too busy getting
ready for his trick.

He appeared to be doing something
behind the table.

"I shall now say the magic word," he announced, tapping the mound under the handkerchief with his wand. "ABRA-CA-DABRA!"

As Paddington tapped at the handkerchief a murmur of approval went round
the audience, for sure enough, the egg had
disappeared.

"Bravo!" shouted Mr. Gruber.
"Good old Paddington!" cried Judy.

But Paddington was far from finished. Before the applause for the first half of his trick had died away he raised his hat and withdrew a bunch of roses.

Mr. Brown took a closer look at the crumpled objects in Paddington's paw. "Aren't those my roses?" he exclaimed.

"No wonder the bushes looked rather bare just now!"

"Shh, Henry," said Mrs. Brown. "I'm sure they'll straighten out again once they're in water.

"Besides, I think he's about to do another trick."

"Perhaps he's going to make himself disappear now," said Judy.

Everyone waited patiently for something to happen, but as the minutes ticked by they looked more and more uneasy.

"Do you think young Mr. Brown's all right in there?" asked Mr. Gruber at last.

"No, I'm not," cried Paddington. "It's all dark and I can't read my instructions."

Mr. Gruber hurried to Paddington's assistance.

"If I were you," he said, as Paddington crawled out, "I would try something simpler next time."

"Hear! Hear!" called Mr. Curry.
"I didn't think much of that trick. I'd like to see something else."

Paddington thanked his friend and then peered at the instruction book again.

"There's a very good one here to do with a watch," he announced at last.

At the mention of the word "watch", everyone hastily pulled their cuffs down over their wrists. All, that is, except Mr. Curry, who had just spied a plate of sandwiches which had been overlooked.

"You wanted to see another trick," said Mrs. Bird pointedly. "Now's your chance!"

"Very well," said Mr. Curry with ill grace. "But make sure you look after it, bear. It's very valuable."

Paddington placed Mr. Curry's watch on the table, covered it carefully with the handkerchief, and then picked up a large mallet.

"This is a very good trick," he announced, as he hit the handkerchief several times as hard as he could. "It says so in the book."

"Now," continued Paddington. "I will lift up the corner of the handkerchief . . . so, and . . . oh! Oh, dear!"

"Oh, dear!" bellowed Mr. Curry.
"What do you mean . . . *oh, dear*?
What's happened, bear?"

Out of the corner of his eye Paddington caught sight of some ominous words in his book of instructions. "For this trick," it said, "it is necessary to use a *dummy* watch."

"I think perhaps I forgot to say ABRACADABRA, Mr. Curry," he faltered.

"ABRACADABRA!" thundered Mr. Curry as he stared at the remains of his watch. "ABRACADABRA! I'll give you ABRACADABRA! That was a very valuable antique. It was shockproof, *and* it had twenty jewels."

"It doesn't look very shockproof to me," said Mr. Brown.

"And it certainly isn't valuable," said Mr. Gruber. "Old it may be, but it's not an antique. I remember selling it to you years ago and you didn't pay me much for it then."

"I think I may have found one of the jewels, Mr. Curry," said Paddington excitedly.

"*One* of the jewels!" exclaimed Mr. Curry. "What about the other nineteen? This is disgraceful!"

Mr. Curry was so cross he flung himself down in his chair, and just as quickly he leapt up again. "Ugh!" he said. "I'm sitting on something sticky!"

"Oh, dear," said Paddington. "I think you've sat on my disappearing egg, Mr. Curry. It must have reappeared again!"

"Serves you right for telling lies to a young bear," said Mrs. Bird sternly. "Trying to make him think it was a valuable watch indeed!"

"Pah!" snorted Mr. Curry.

But for once the Browns' neighbour was at a loss for words. "I shall never." he said, glaring at Paddington as he made for the door, "ever come to one of your parties again!"

When the laughter had died down, Mr. Brown looked at his own watch. "It's getting very near bedtime," he said. "Most of all Paddington's, so I suggest we *all* do a disappearing trick now!"

"All good things come to an end," said Judy, as she and Jonathan joined Paddington on the doorstep of number thirty-two Windsor Gardens while he waved goodbye to everyone. "Even birthday parties."

"If they didn't," said Jonathan, "you'd never have another one to look forward to."

"Perhaps," said Paddington, as he went upstairs to bed. "I'd better write this one up in my scrapbook first before I forget it.

"Besides, I want to tell my Aunt Lucy all about it, and so much has happened I may have a job getting it all on one postcard!"

*This story comes from A BEAR CALLED PADDINGTON
and is based on the television film. It has been
specially written by Michael Bond for
younger children.*

ISBN 0 00 123207 X (paperback)
ISBN 0 00 123214 2 (cased)
Text copyright © 1977 Michael Bond
Illustrations copyright © 1977 William Collins Sons & Co. Ltd.
Cover copyright © 1977 William Collins Sons & Co. Ltd. and Film Fair Ltd.
Cover design by Ivor Wood. Cover photographed by Bruce Scott.
Printed in Great Britain